*To Charles*

A catalogue record for this book is available from the British Library

Published by Ladybird Books Ltd  Loughborough  Leicestershire  UK
Ladybird Books Ltd is a subsidiary of the Penguin Group of companies
© LADYBIRD BOOKS LTD MCMXCVI

# Fly Eagle Fly!

by *Jan Pollard*
*illustrated by* Martine Gourbault

Let me sit on your back, great eagle,
and fly me across the seas,
where the ocean roars on distant shores
and parrots live in trees.

We'll watch whales when they break through
the surface of the deep and restless sea,
as they leap in the air and plunge downwards,
with their huge tails pointing at me.

Let us swoop through the valleys, great eagle,
where no one has been before...

and fly over the tops of the mountains,
where the vultures and condors soar.

Fly me over the lonely deserts,
where the sand dunes ripple like sea,
and nomads riding their camels
look up and wave to me.

Show me lands that are teeming with people...

and lands that are water and ice...

and forests...

and plains where it seldom rains...

and people in fields, planting rice.

Let us listen to temple bells ringing
as we fly over rooftops of gold...

and see bullocks pulling the ploughshare
and turning the earth, as of old.

We shall stand on the tallest building,
with people and cars far below,
looking like ants in an ant's nest,
scurrying to and fro.

Let us look at the mighty icebergs
as they move through the arctic seas,
and watch bears as they walk on the ice floes
in waters that always freeze.

Take me to see the green jungle,
where the canopy keeps out the sun,
and where tigers prowl and monkeys howl
and swing in the treetops for fun.

Find rocks where waterfalls tumble
and colours shine in each drop,
so we'll have a rainbow to fly through
before we are ready to stop.

Let me down gently, great eagle,
when our long journey is done.
I'll remember the people and places we've seen,
and think of them, one by one.